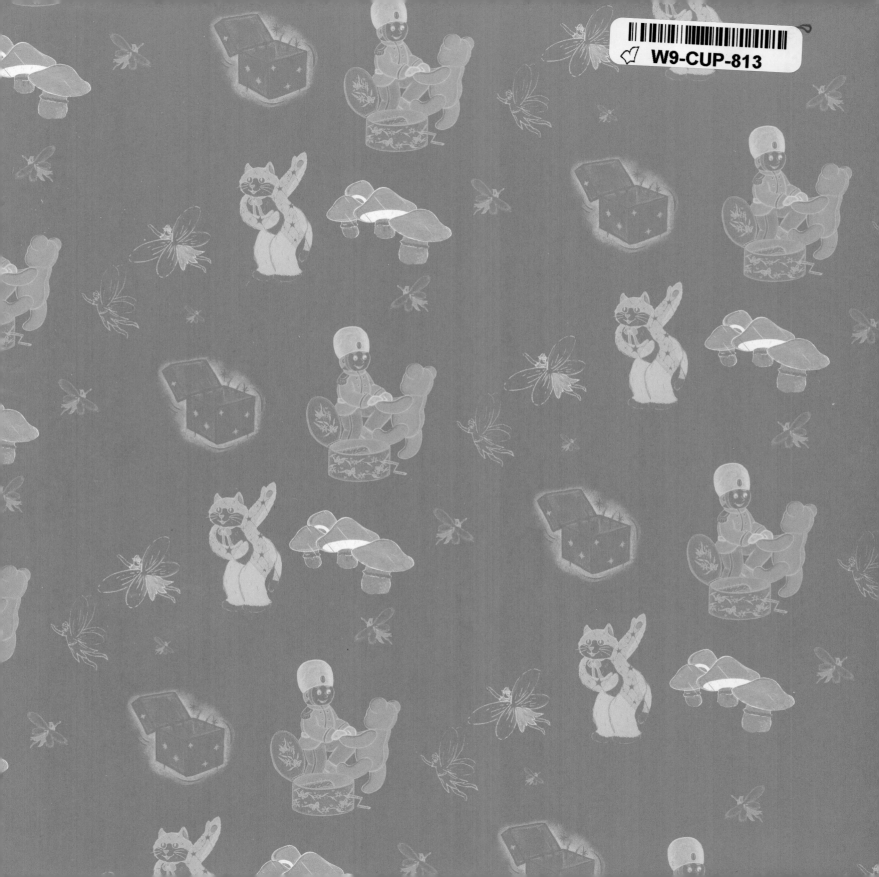

The House
in the Tree
~ & ~
The
Strange
Doll

Published in 2005 by Mercury Junior
20 Bloomsbury Street, London WC1B 3JH

© text copyright Enid Blyton Limited
© copyright original illustrations, Hodder and Stoughton Limited
© new illustrations 2005 Mercury Junior

Designed and produced for Mercury Junior
by Open Door Limited, Langham, Rutland

Title: The House in the Tree & The Strange Doll
ISBN: 1 904668 37 2

The House in the Tree

~ & ~

The Strange Doll

Mercury
Junior

The House in the Tree

Eileen and Marigold lived next door to one another, and they played together every day. But they were quite different!

Eileen was lazy and wouldn't bother about anything. Marigold liked to work hard, and would help anyone she could. Eileen was eight and Marigold was seven.

Eileen couldn't read and Marigold could.

Eileen didn't even know her twice times table, but Marigold had already got as far as four times.

Eileen laughed at Marigold because she liked doing things. "You are silly to learn to read," she said. "Your mother won't read to you any more now."

"Oh yes, she will," said Marigold, "and I'll be able to read to myself, too, so I'll get twice as many stories!"

"Well, I can always get my mother to read to me whenever I want a story," said Eileen.

"So what's the use of bothering to learn?"

"You are lazy," said Marigold. "You can't even knit, as I can – you can't even tie a bow!"

"Well, you couldn't last week!" said Eileen.

"But I can now," said Marigold. "Look – I tied my own shoe-laces this morning – one on each foot. It took me a long time, but I did it. Now I can tie them every morning."

"Pooh!" said Eileen, scornfully. "I can get my mother to tie mine in half the time. What's the use of learning that if you've got someone to do it for you?"

Now one day, when Eileen and Marigold were playing in the wood, they heard the sound of someone squealing.

"Oooh! Oooh! Now look what I've done!"

Eileen and Marigold peeped round a tree to see who was squealing – and they saw a plump little woman sitting on a tree-trunk sucking her hand.

"What have you done?" asked Marigold.

"I was chopping wood for my fire when the chopper cut my thumb," said the little woman, her bright eyes twinkling at Marigold. "I shall have to bandage it."

"I'll do it for you," said Marigold. She took her clean hanky from her pocket and tore it into neat strips for a bandage. Then she quickly bound the little woman's thumb, and tied a neat little bow.

"What beautiful bows you tie," said the little woman, looking at her bandage. "Thank you very much. My goodness, my thumb does hurt. I don't believe I'll be able to dress my children for their party this afternoon!"

"Shall we help you?" asked Marigold.

"I don't want to," said Eileen, who was feeling lazy. "I want to play."

"Can you tie bows?" the little lady asked her, and Eileen shook her head. "Well, it's no use coming to help dress my children if you can't tie bows, because their party dresses have sashes – and they have to be tied in beautiful bows and each child has two plaits with bows at the end. So you wouldn't be any help. But this little girl would be a great help. Come along in, my dear!"

"Where's your house?" asked Marigold, looking round.

"In here!" said the little woman, and she pressed a bit of bark on a great oak-tree. A round door swung open! Marigold stared in surprise. So did Eileen.

The little woman went in at the door and pulled Marigold in too.

The door shut with a bang.

There was such a dear little room inside the tree. It was quite round. There was a table in the middle and a wooden seat ran all round. Seven small pixie children were sitting on the seat, as quiet as mice.

"Oh!" said Marigold, "Your children are fairies!" "Yes," said the little woman, and

she shook out a pair
of wings from under
her shawl.

"I'm a pixie too,
but I usually cover
up my wings in the
wood in case anyone
sees me. Now, children – get your dresses!"

Each child opened a tiny cupboard beneath
the seat where she sat and pulled out
gossamer dresses.

They were in two colours – blue and yellow. The blue dresses had yellow sashes and the yellow dresses had blue sashes. Each child had two pieces of hair ribbon to match her sash.

They all wore plaits and looked perfectly sweet.

What a busy time Marigold had! She tied seven sashes into beautiful bows! She tied fourteen hair-ribbons into fourteen bows on the ends of fourteen little plaits! The children were as good as gold. Their mother was so grateful to Marigold.

"I suppose you wouldn't take the children to their party for me, would you?" she asked. "My hurt thumb really makes me feel rather ill."

"Oh, I'd love to!" said Marigold at once. "Where is the party?"

"It is at the Princess Silvertoes' palace in the heart of the wood," said the little woman. "The children know the way. Tell the Princess about my thumb, won't you, and say I'm sorry I cannot come. Good-bye, dears!"

They all went out of the tree. Eileen was still outside, wondering what had happened to Marigold. When she saw her coming out with seven beautifully dressed pixies she was most surprised.

"I'm taking these pixies to a party at Princess Silvertoes', in the heart of the wood," said Marigold to Eileen. "Go home and tell Mother I will be a bit late."

"I want to come too," said Eileen in excitement. "Well, you can't" said the pixies' mother, standing in the doorway.

"You didn't want to help me at all. You can't

even tie a bow! You are a lazy, good-for-nothing little girl, and I don't want you to go with my children. Go home!"

So whilst Marigold went to the party and had a wonderful time, poor Eileen had to go home in tears.

And I shouldn't be surprised if she learnt to tie a bow the very next day!

I hope you can tie a bow – you never know when it will come in useful, do you?

The Strange Doll

Doreen was very sad. She had a lovely baby doll that could shut its eyes and could say "Mama" quite plainly – and now the doll was broken!

It wasn't really Doreen's fault. She had put it on the table in the kitchen just for a moment whilst she went to get her doll's pram – and Mummy hadn't seen it there. She had put down a tray of dirty cups and saucers, and the doll had fallen off the table.

Crash! Her pretty face broke into pieces, and both her legs broke, too.

Doreen was very much upset and cried bitterly.

"Oh, Mummy, can't she be mended?" she asked.

But Mummy shook her head. "No, I don't think so," she said. "She is too much broken. I'm afraid I can't buy you another doll just yet, darling, because I really haven't the money.

You must wait for your birthday."

"But that's ever such a long time away," said poor Doreen. "Oh Mummy, I shan't have a doll to take out in my pram now!"

Doreen put the broken doll in the pram cupboard. Then she put her pram away – but when she took hold of the handle, she thought she would go down the lane to the farm and back again, even though she had no doll in the pram to wheel along.

She would just pretend!

So off went the little girl, wheeling her empty pram. She went right down to the farm and then just turned to go back again.

Just as she turned, she heard a little whimpering noise. She looked round to see where it was. By the side of the lane, huddled under the hedge, was a puppy-dog. He was crying sadly all to himself.

Doreen went over to him. "What's the matter?" she asked. "Poor little puppy-dog, you are unhappy!"

The little dog whimpered again and did not move. "Come along!" said Doreen. "Come along! Don't sit under the damp hedge. Come out into the road and let me see you!"

But still the puppy did not move. So Doreen picked him up gently – and then she saw that he was hurt! One of his legs was bleeding, and he held it up as if it hurt him very much.

"Oh, dear!" said Doreen. "You're hurt! How did it happen? Did a farm-horse kick you – or a motor-car hurt you?"

The puppy whimpered again and licked Doreen on the face. He thought she was a dear, kind little girl.

She put him down on the ground and tried to make him walk after her – but he was very much frightened, and would not move a step.

Doreen remembered that dogs have their names on their collars, so she took hold of his pretty red collar and looked at it. On it was printed: "White Cottage, Elmers End."

"Oh, you belong to Mrs. Harrison, who lives at Elmers End!" said Doreen. "Oh, dear – that's a long way away! I wonder if you can possibly get there."

The puppy yelped. He was trying to tell Doreen what had happened.

His mistress had driven her car to the farm that morning and, just as she was leaving again, he had jumped out and hurt his leg. Now he was too frightened to do anything at all.

"However can I get you back?" said Doreen, patting the soft little head. "Oh! I've got such a good idea! I'll put you in my doll's pram, puppy! My doll broke this morning, poor thing, and the pram is empty. You'll fit in there nicely, because you are so small. I think I can manage to walk all the way to Mrs. Harrison's."

She picked up the puppy dog and put him gently into the doll's pram.

He snuggled down on the pillow happily.

It felt like his soft basket at home! Doreen pulled the covers over him and told him to go to sleep.

And so tired and frightened was the poor little puppy that he really did close his eyes and fall asleep in the pram!
Doreen was so pleased.

"It's almost as good as having a doll!"
she thought. Off she went, wheeling
her pram carefully so as not to wake up the
sleeping puppy-dog.

It was a long way to White Cottage where Mrs. Harrison lived. The little girl's legs were very tired long before she got there, but she didn't stop for a moment. She did so badly want to get the puppy back to his home and tell Mrs. Harrison to bathe his leg and wrap it up.

At last she came to White Cottage. Mrs. Harrison was in the garden, cutting roses. She looked up in surprise as she saw Doreen wheeling her pram up the path.

"Good morning, dear!" she called. "Have you come to show me your baby doll? What a long way you must have walked! You look quite tired!"

She went over to the pram and peeped inside – and how astonished she was to see a

sleeping puppy there
– her own puppy too!
She stared and stared!

"Why, it's Sammy!" she said. "I thought I had left him behind at the farm and I was going to fetch him this afternoon!"

"I found him just near the farm, with a hurt leg," said Doreen. "I hadn't a doll in my pram to-day, because it got broken this morning.

I was very sad about it because Mummy said it couldn't be mended, and she can't buy me another doll till my birthday. So I took my pram out empty – and it was a good thing I did, really, because, you see, when I found poor Sammy, I could put him into the empty pram and wheel him all the way home to you. I think his leg wants bathing and bandaging, Mrs. Harrison."

What a to-do there was then! The puppy woke up and tried to jump out of the pram when it saw its mistress. Its leg hurt and it yelped. Mrs. Harrison called for warm water and an old handkerchief – and soon the little dog's leg was well bathed and had a nice clean bandage on.

He really looked quite proud of it.

"Well, now, my dear, it really is time for your dinner," said Mrs. Harrison, looking at the clock. "Good gracious! It's past one o'clock! Your mother will be worrying about you. I'll run you and your pram home in the car."

She took out her little brown car and popped the pram into the back seat. Doreen sat in the front and in a very little while they were back at Doreen's home.

Mrs. Harrison explained to Doreen's mother how kind the little girl had been.

"She tells me her baby doll was broken this morning and that was how it came about that her pram was empty and she could take Sammy back to me," said Mrs. Harrison.

"I was sorry to hear about her doll. Do give it to me, Mrs. White, for I am sure I can get it mended for her. I know a doll's hospital in the next town. I can get a nice new head and two new legs put on, I'm sure."

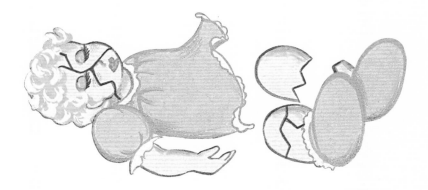

She took the doll away with her and – will you believe it – in three days she brought it back again, quite better! It had on a lovely new head, just as nice as the first one, and two beautiful fat legs. The doll smiled at Doreen, who hugged it and kissed it in delight.

"Oh, thank you, Mrs. Harrison!" she said. "You are kind!"

"Well, you were kind first!" said Mrs. Harrison, with a smile. "It's funny how things happen, isn't it? Your doll got broken – so you took your pram out empty – and found Sammy and put him into it – and I was pleased, and heard about your broken doll and wanted to get it mended for you! So your bit of kindness has come back to you and made you happy! I'm glad!"

But the gladdest person of all was Doreen, as you can guess!